Library of Congress Catalog Card Number 82-45860
ISBN: 0-385-17815-8

Library of Congress Cataloging in Publication Data

Gantz, David.
  Captain Swifty and his happy hearts band.

  Summary: Captain Swifty and his friends form their
own band out of home-made instruments and demonstrate
a variety of sounds.
  [1. Musical instruments—Fiction. 2. Animals—
Fiction] I. Title.
PZ7.G1535Can 1983   [E]

Captain Swifty and His Happy Hearts Band

A Book About SOUNDS

by David Gantz

Doubleday & Company, Inc., Garden City, New York

One Sunday morning Captain
Swifty was sitting on a tree
stump, fishing in Crescent Bay.

Calico Cat was tossing pebbles in the water, and at first the Captain was annoyed.

The Captain didn't need much time to answer Calico's question.

Since the fish weren't biting, the Captain decided to join Calico.

They were plinking, plunking, and toonking, tossing bigger and bigger rocks and making larger and noisier splashes.

"It's one thing when you drop those silly rusty hooks in my water," said the angry fish. "I can easily ignore that. But when you start pummeling us with rocks, that's too much!"

It was Roscoe Rabbit making sweet sounds on something.

Soon they met Moxy Mouse coming down the road carrying a fiddle case.

Moxy Mouse opened his fiddle case. He had an empty shoe box, some rubber bands and, as always, his ketchup bottle where Genie Bear with the Light Brown Hair lived.

Moxy explained that it was Sunday, Genie Bear's day off, and that he didn't grant wishes on his day off.

Moxy cut a hole in the box top, stuck a stick in its side, and stretched rubber bands across the top of the box to the end of the stick.

Moxy strummed a few notes on his shoebox guitar.

"What are you going to call this band, Captain?"
asked Moxy.

Captain Swifty and his Happy Hearts Band were marching merrily down the road making music . . .

. . . when they came upon Morris the Mailman taking a bath in a tin tub.

Morris nailed an
old mop handle to the
side of his tub . . .

Captain Swifty's Happy Hearts Band was rapidly growing. There was Roscoe Rabbit on the reed flute, Moxy Mouse on the shoe box guitar, Calico Cat on the bucket drum, and Morris the Mailman on the washtub bass.

As they continued on, they heard a sound coming from a thicket.

When they peeked through the brush,
they saw Algernon the Alligator.

"That music," asked Captain Swifty,
"is coming from a chair?"

Sure, see?

Bwing
Bwong
Bwang

Algernon, how would you like to join our string section?

They heard a rattling sound coming from a tree.
When they looked up they saw Squawk shaking two
gourds with handles on them.

Rattle
Rattle
Rattle

The band passed Beulah Beaver's place. Beulah was washing clothes as usual. "How about taking your washboard and joining us?" asked Captain Swifty.

A trumpet sound was coming from the direction of the beach. When they got there, Hepzibah Hippo was blowing on a conch shell.

Captain Swifty and his Happy Hearts Band
were merrily marching along the beach when
they passed the spot where Moxy had left
his ketchup bottle with Genie Bear
sleeping inside.

Rattle
Rattle
Rattle
Bam
Bop
Bam
Plinkity
Plank
Plunk
Twiddle
dee
Tweet

Suddenly, they heard
a very familiar
voice say . . .